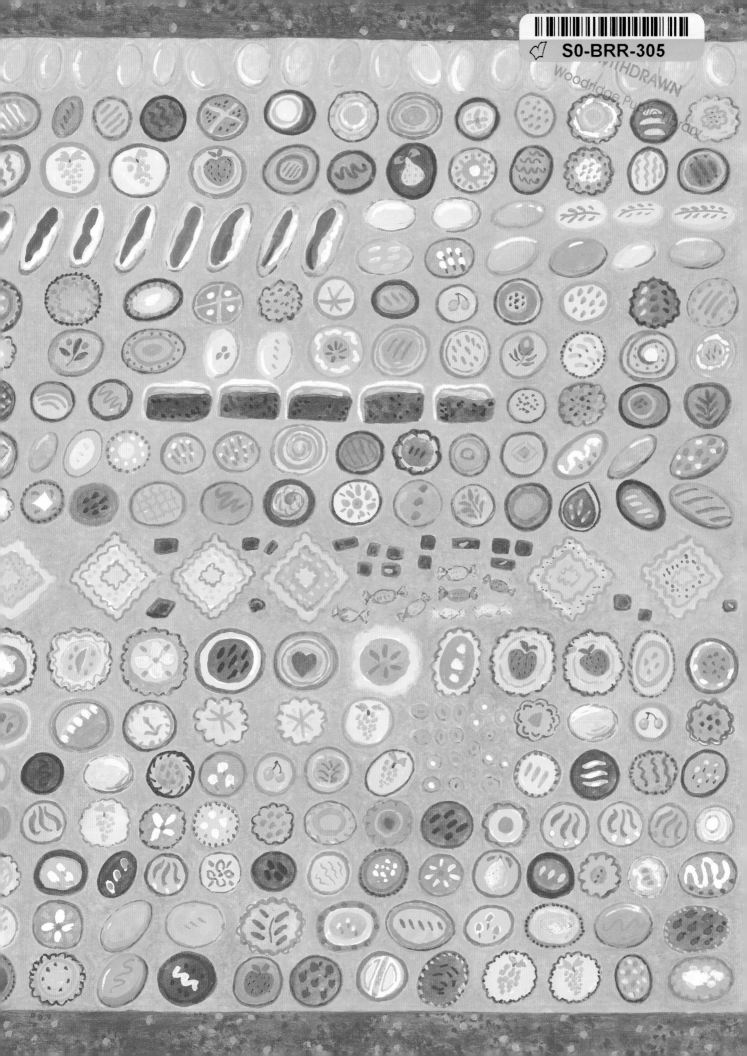

Hansel
and
Gretel

Illustrations copyright © 1987, 2018 by NordSüd Verlag AG, CH-8005 Zürich, Switzerland.
This edition first published in 2018 by NorthSouth Books Inc., New York 10016.

First published in the United States, Great Britain, Canada, Australia, and New Zealand in 2018 by NorthSouth Books Inc., an imprint of NordSüd Verlag AG, CH-8005 Zürich, Switzerland.

Distributed in the United States by NorthSouth Books Inc., New York 10016.
Library of Congress Cataloging-in-Publication Data is available.
ISBN: 978-0-7358-4327-1
Printed in Latvia
1 3 5 7 9 • 10 8 6 4 2
www.northsouth.com

Bernadette Watts

Hansel and Gretel

Based on a fairy tale by The Brothers Grimm

North
South

Once upon a time on the edge of a large forest there lived a poor woodcutter with his wife and his two children. The little boy was called Hansel, and the little girls was called Gretel. They had very little to eat, and when a terrible famine hit the land, they had hardly enough to bake a loaf of bread.

One evening, as he was sitting worrying by the fire, his wife said to him, "I tell you what we will have to do. First thing tomorrow we will take the children out into the thickest part of the forest. There we will make a fire and give them each a piece of bread, then we can go about our work and leave them behind. They won't find their way back home, and we will be rid of them."

But the wife called him a fool and said, "Then we must all four starve to death, and you can cut the wood for our coffins." She gave him no peace until he gave in.

The two children had not been able to go to sleep because they were so hungry and had heard what their stepmother had said to their father. Hansel comforted Gretel, then slipped outside and collected as many white pebbles that shone in the moonlight as would fit into his pocket. Then he went back in again and spoke to Gretel. "Don't worry, sleep in peace; God will look after us," he said, and got back into bed.

When the day broke, even before the sun had risen, their stepmother came and woke the two children. "Get up, lazybones; we are going into the forest to fetch some wood."

Then she gave each of them a piece of bread and said, "Here is something for your lunch. Don't eat it straightaway, for you won't get any more."

Gretel put the bread in her apron pocket, because Hansel had the stones in his. After they had been walking awhile, Hansel stopped and looked back toward the house.

His father said, "Hansel, what are you looking at?"

"Oh, Father," said Hansel, "I am looking at my little white cat, which is sitting on the roof. He wants to say good-bye to me."

"Don't be silly," said his stepmother; "it is just the morning sun shining on the chimney."

However, Hansel hadn't really been looking at the cat but had been dropping some of the little white pebbles on the path.

When they were deep in the forest, they gathered some twigs and lit a fire. Their stepmother said, "Now, lie down by the fire and have a rest. We are going farther into the forest to cut some wood. We will be back to fetch you as soon as we have finished."

Hansel and Gretel sat by the fire and ate their bread. After they had been waiting a long time, their eyes closed and they fell asleep. When they finally awoke, it was late at night. Gretel started crying, but Hansel comforted her, saying, "We must wait until the full moon is out, then we will easily find the way home." He took his sister by the hand and started following the pebbles, which were shining like new pennies. By dawn they were back home.

Not long afterwards, they were once again in dire need, and so the step-mother said to the father, "Everything has been eaten up and all that's left is half a loaf. We must take the children deeper into the forest so they cannot possibly find their way back. There is no other way we shall be saved." Again the father didn't want to do it, but because he had given in the first time, he had to do so again for the second time.

However, the children were still awake and had overheard the conversation. When the old people had gone to sleep, Hansel got up and tried to go out to collect pebbles as he had done previously, but the doors had been locked by their stepmother. Hansel comforted his sister, saying, "Don't worry; God will help us. In the morning I will break little bits off my bread and throw them on the path. Then we will be able to find our way home."

The next day the children were taken farther out into the forest, deeper than they had ever been before. A fire was lit, and the two old people went to cut wood. Gretel shared her bread with Hansel, and then they fell asleep. No one came to the poor children, and when they awoke it was late at night. They warmed their hands over the fire, and Hansel comforted his sister, saying, "Wait until the moon is out, and then we will see the scraps of bread that I have scattered along the path. They will show us the way home."

When the moon rose, they started off; but they could not find any of the pieces of bread, for the birds had eaten them all. Hansel said to Gretel, "We will soon find the path," but they couldn't. They walked the whole night and the following day, but they couldn't get out of the forest. The next day, they saw a beautiful snow-white bird sitting on a twig. It was singing so beautifully that they stopped to listen to it. When it had finished, it flapped its wings and flew in front of them. They followed it until they came across a little house, on whose roof the bird landed.

When they went closer, they could see that the house was built of
bread and decorated with cakes. The windows were made of clear
sugar.

"Let's get our teeth into it and have a lovely meal," said Hansel, and
broke off a piece of the roof. Gretel stood by the door and started
nibbling.

Then a voice called from the window:

"Nibble, nibble, mousekin,

Who's nibbling at my housekin?"

The children answered:

"The breeze, the breeze

That blows through the trees."

and ate on without letting it worry them.

All of a sudden the door opened, and a woman as old as the hills crept out. Hansel and Gretel were frightened. The old woman took them both by the hand and led them inside. "Do come in and stay with me," she said. "You will come to no harm." She brought them some lovely food, milk, and pancakes with sugar, apples, and nuts.

But the next morning, before the children were awake, the old woman got up; and as she looked sweetly at the two children with their rosy cheeks, she murmured to herself, "They will make a tasty mouthful." You see, the old woman was really a wicked witch who waylaid children so that she could eat them. She had built the little house of gingerbread merely to tempt them in.

She seized Hansel in her scrawny hands and put him in a little cage, and locked him in behind a wire door. He could scream as much as he liked and it would do him no good. Then she went to Gretel, shook her awake, and said, "Get up, lazybones, and cook your brother something nice to fatten him up. Then I can eat him."

Gretel cried bitterly, but she had to do what the wicked witch demanded. The best food was cooked for poor Hansel, but Gretel got nothing but crab shells. Every morning, the old woman crept to the cage and cried, "Hansel, stick your finger out so that I can feel how fat you are." But Hansel poked a little bone out, and the old woman, who had bad eyesight and couldn't see properly, thought it was Hansel's finger and wondered why he wasn't getting any fatter.

After four weeks were up and Hansel was just as thin as ever, the old witch became so impatient that she couldn't wait any longer. "Hey, Gretel," she shouted to the girl, "stir yourself and fetch some water. I don't care if Hansel is fat or thin; tomorrow I am going to kill him and cook him." When Gretel started crying, the old woman said, "Just keep your noise to yourself; it won't help you at all."

Early the next morning, Gretel had to go out and fetch some wood.

"First I am going to do some baking," said the old woman. "I have already heated up the oven and kneaded the dough." She pushed poor Gretel toward the oven, out of which flames were already shooting. "Creep in," said the witch, "and see if it is burning properly so that we can put the bread in." As soon as Gretel was inside, she was going to shut the oven and bake Gretel so that she could eat her too.

But Gretel realized what the old woman had in mind and said, "I am not sure what I have to do. How do I get in?"

"Silly goose," said the old woman, "the opening is quite big enough. Look—even I can get in," and with that she put her head into the oven.

Then Gretel gave her a push so that she toppled in. She quickly shut the iron door and shot the bolt. With frightful screams and shouts, the old woman was burned to death. Gretel was a bit shaken but quickly ran to Hansel and freed him from his cage, and the two joyfully fell into each other's arms.

Now that the witch was burned, the two had nothing to fear. They took all the pearls and jewels from the chests that stood in every corner.

"These are better than pebbles," said Hansel, and filled his bag as full as possible.

Then they set off out of the witch's wood. But after they had
been walking a few hours, they came across a large pond.
"There are neither stepping- stones nor a bridge," said Gretel;
"but a white swan is swimming over there, and if I ask him, he
will help us across." So she called out:

"Little swan, little swan, please come near,
Hansel and Gretel are waiting here.
There's not a stone or a bridge in sight.
Please take us across on your back so white."

And the swan swam to her and carried the two children one
after the other across the water.

After they had been walking for a while, they came to a part of the forest that they recognized, and finally from far off they saw their father's house. The poor man hadn't had a moment's peace since he had left the children in the forest. By now his wife had died, and he was living alone. When they arrived, he hugged them joyfully, and with the pearls and jewels that the children shook out of their bags, they all lived happily ever after.

My tale is over, there runs a mouse; whoever catches it may make himself a great big fur cap out of it.